THIS GARDEN THEMED
NOT QUITE CUSSING
Coloring Book
FOR ADULTS

BELONGS TO:

....

DATE:

....

© Leafy Design

All rights reserved. No part of this publication may be reproduced, distributed or transmitted in any form or by any means including photocopying, recording or other electronic methods without the prior written permission of the publisher.

NOT QUITE CUSSING COLORING BOOK

© Leafy Design. All rights reserved. No part of this publication may be reproduced, distributed or transmitted in any form or by any means including photocopying, recording or other electronic methods without the prior written permission of the publisher.

OH MY Gourd!

NOT QUITE CUSSING COLORING BOOK

© Leafy Design. All rights reserved. No part of this publication may be reproduced, distributed or transmitted in any form or by any means including photocopying, recording or other electronic methods without the prior written permission of the publisher.

AW, SHUCKS

NOT QUITE CUSSING COLORING BOOK

© Leafy Design. All rights reserved. No part of this publication may be reproduced, distributed or transmitted in any form or by any means including photocopying, recording or other electronic methods without the prior written permission of the publisher.

I DON'T GIVE A FORK

NOT QUITE CUSSING COLORING BOOK

© Leafy Design. All rights reserved. No part of this publication may be reproduced, distributed or transmitted in any form or by any means including photocopying, recording or other electronic methods without the prior written permission of the publisher.

SON OF A *Peach!*

NOT QUITE CUSSING COLORING BOOK

© Leafy Design. All rights reserved. No part of this publication may be reproduced, distributed or transmitted in any form or by any means including photocopying, recording or other electronic methods without the prior written permission of the publisher.

MIND YOUR GNOME BUSINESS

NOT QUITE CUSSING COLORING BOOK

© Leafy Design. All rights reserved. No part of this publication may be reproduced, distributed or transmitted in any form or by any means including photocopying, recording or other electronic methods without the prior written permission of the publisher.

PUCKER UP

Buttercup

NOT QUITE CUSSING COLORING BOOK

© Leafy Design. All rights reserved. No part of this publication may be reproduced, distributed or transmitted in any form or by any means including photocopying, recording or other electronic methods without the prior written permission of the publisher.

For Crying out Cloud!

NOT QUITE CUSSING COLORING BOOK

© Leafy Design. All rights reserved. No part of this publication may be reproduced, distributed or transmitted in any form or by any means including photocopying, recording or other electronic methods without the prior written permission of the publisher.

YOU BIG BOKWOMBLE

NOT QUITE CUSSING COLORING BOOK

© Leafy Design. All rights reserved. No part of this publication may be reproduced, distributed or transmitted in any form or by any means including photocopying, recording or other electronic methods without the prior written permission of the publisher.

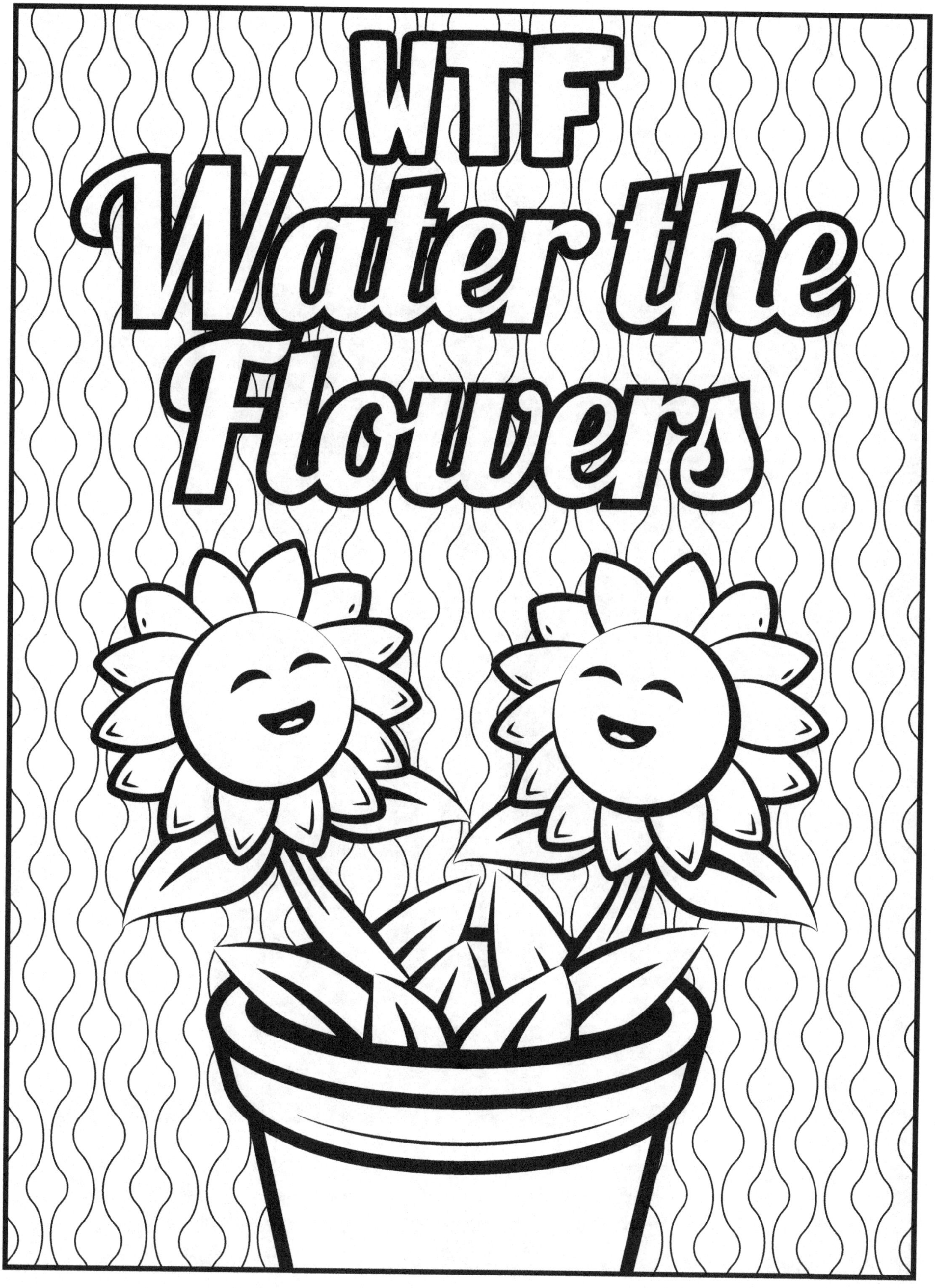
WTF
Water the
Flowers

NOT QUITE CUSSING COLORING BOOK

© Leafy Design. All rights reserved. No part of this publication may be reproduced, distributed or transmitted in any form or by any means including photocopying, recording or other electronic methods without the prior written permission of the publisher.

HOLY SHITTAKE!

NOT QUITE CUSSING COLORING BOOK

© Leafy Design. All rights reserved. No part of this publication may be reproduced, distributed or transmitted in any form or by any means including photocopying, recording or other electronic methods without the prior written permission of the publisher.

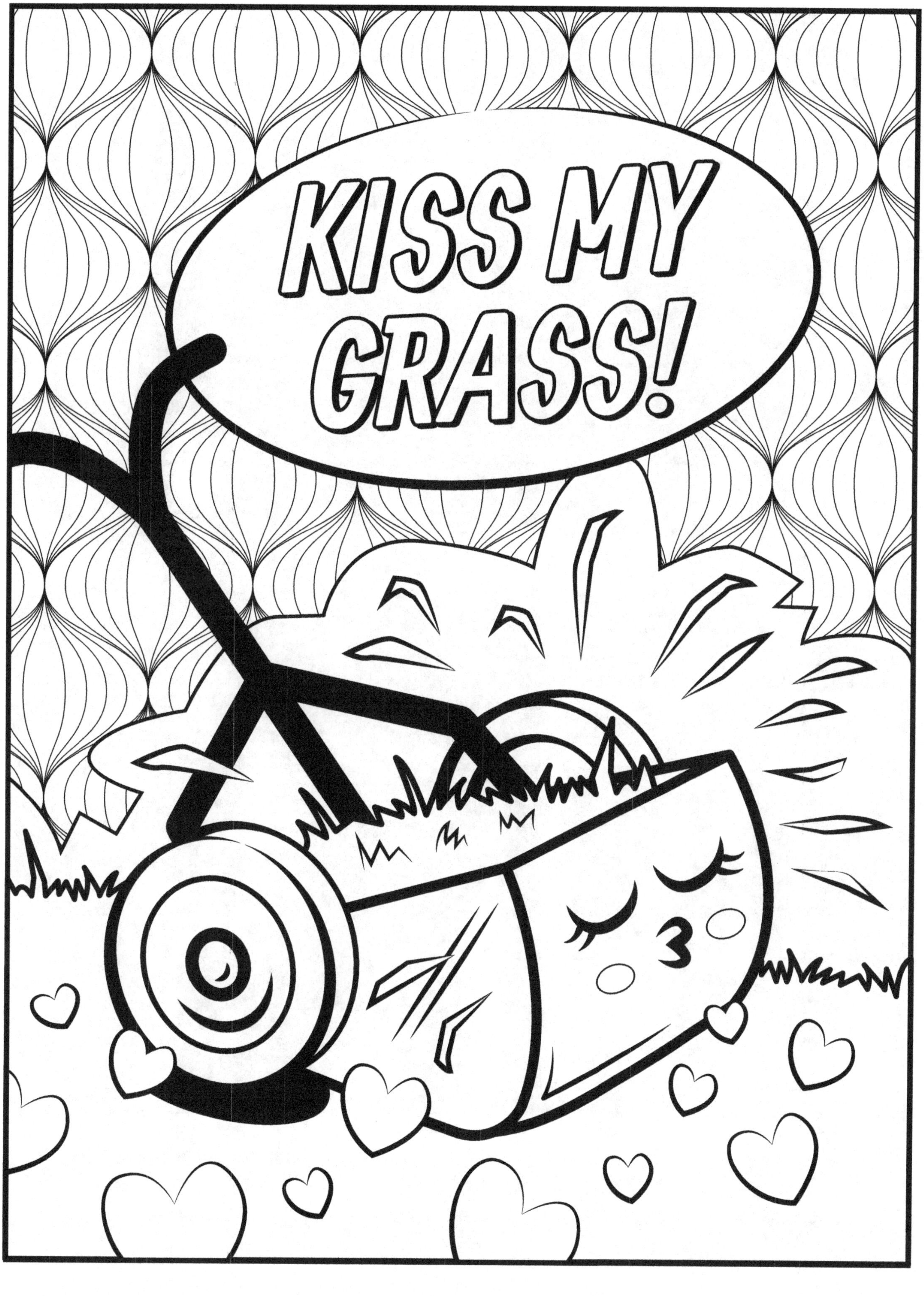
KISS MY GRASS!

NOT QUITE CUSSING COLORING BOOK

© Leafy Design. All rights reserved. No part of this publication may be reproduced, distributed or transmitted in any form or by any means including photocopying, recording or other electronic methods without the prior written permission of the publisher.

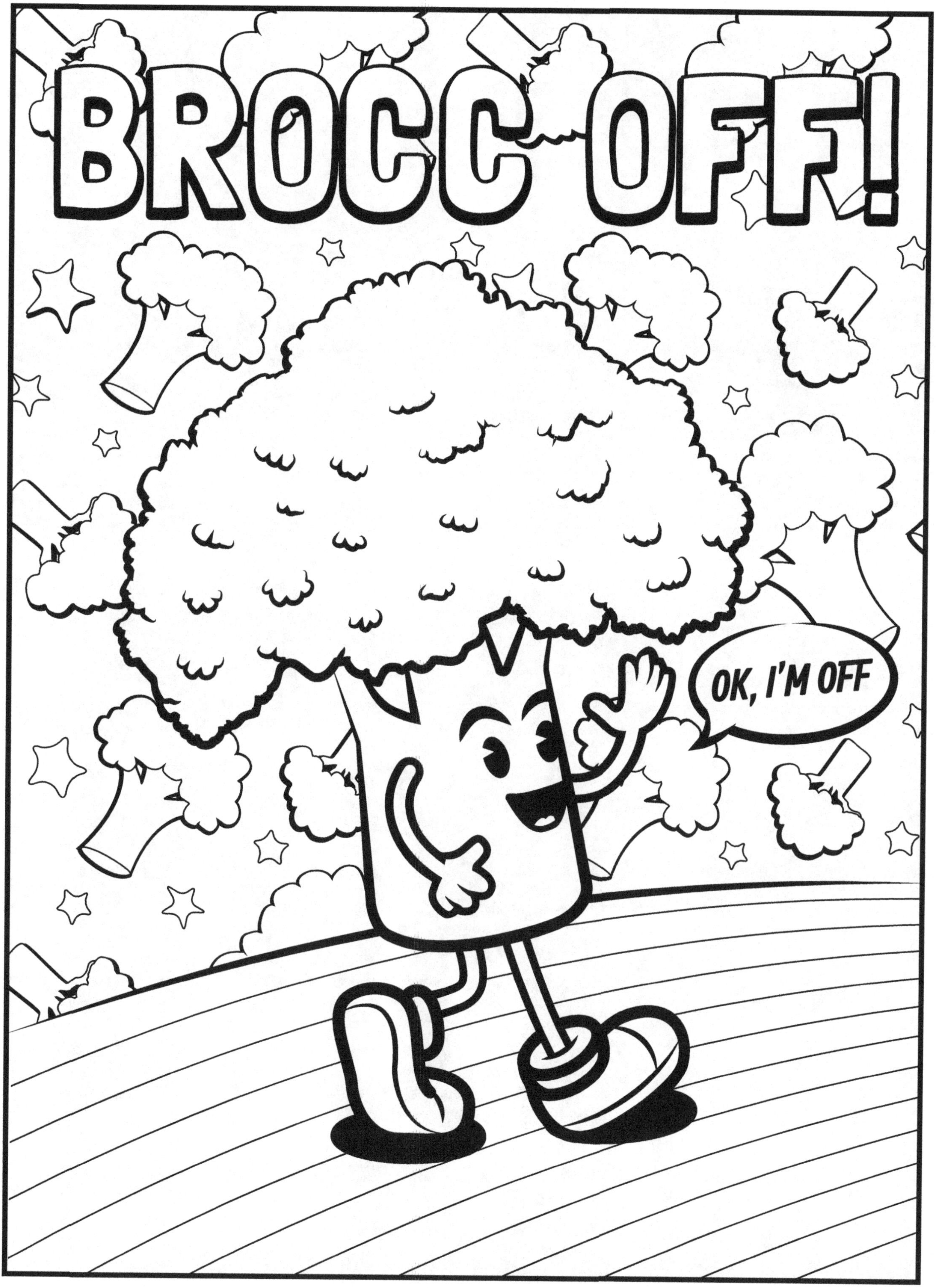
BROCC OFF!
OK, I'M OFF

NOT QUITE CUSSING COLORING BOOK

© Leafy Design. All rights reserved. No part of this publication may be reproduced, distributed or transmitted in any form or by any means including photocopying, recording or other electronic methods without the prior written permission of the publisher.

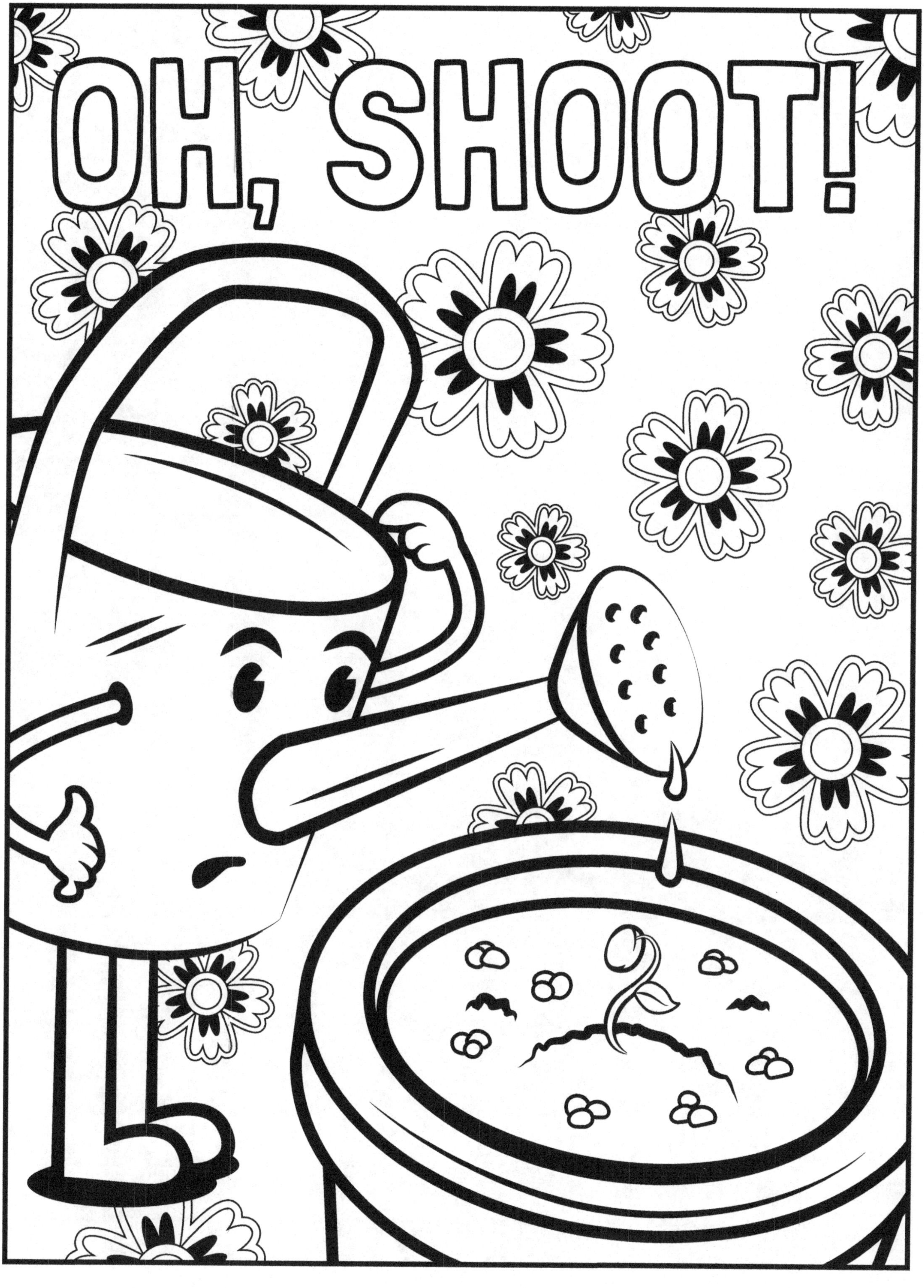
OH, SHOOT!

NOT QUITE CUSSING COLORING BOOK

© Leafy Design. All rights reserved. No part of this publication may be reproduced, distributed or transmitted in any form or by any means including photocopying, recording or other electronic methods without the prior written permission of the publisher.

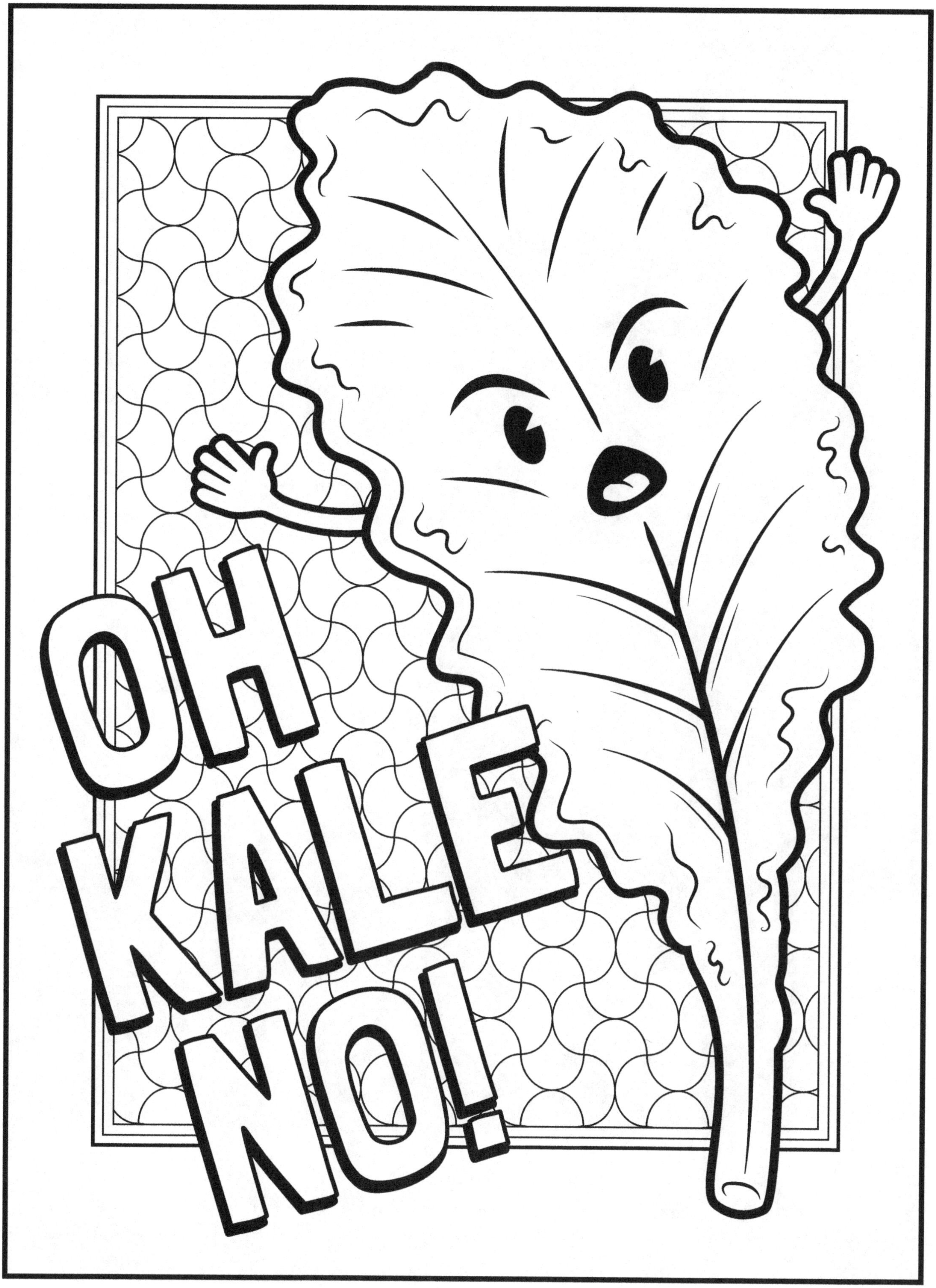
OH
KALE
NO!

NOT QUITE CUSSING COLORING BOOK

© Leafy Design. All rights reserved. No part of this publication may be reproduced, distributed or transmitted in any form or by any means including photocopying, recording or other electronic methods without the prior written permission of the publisher.

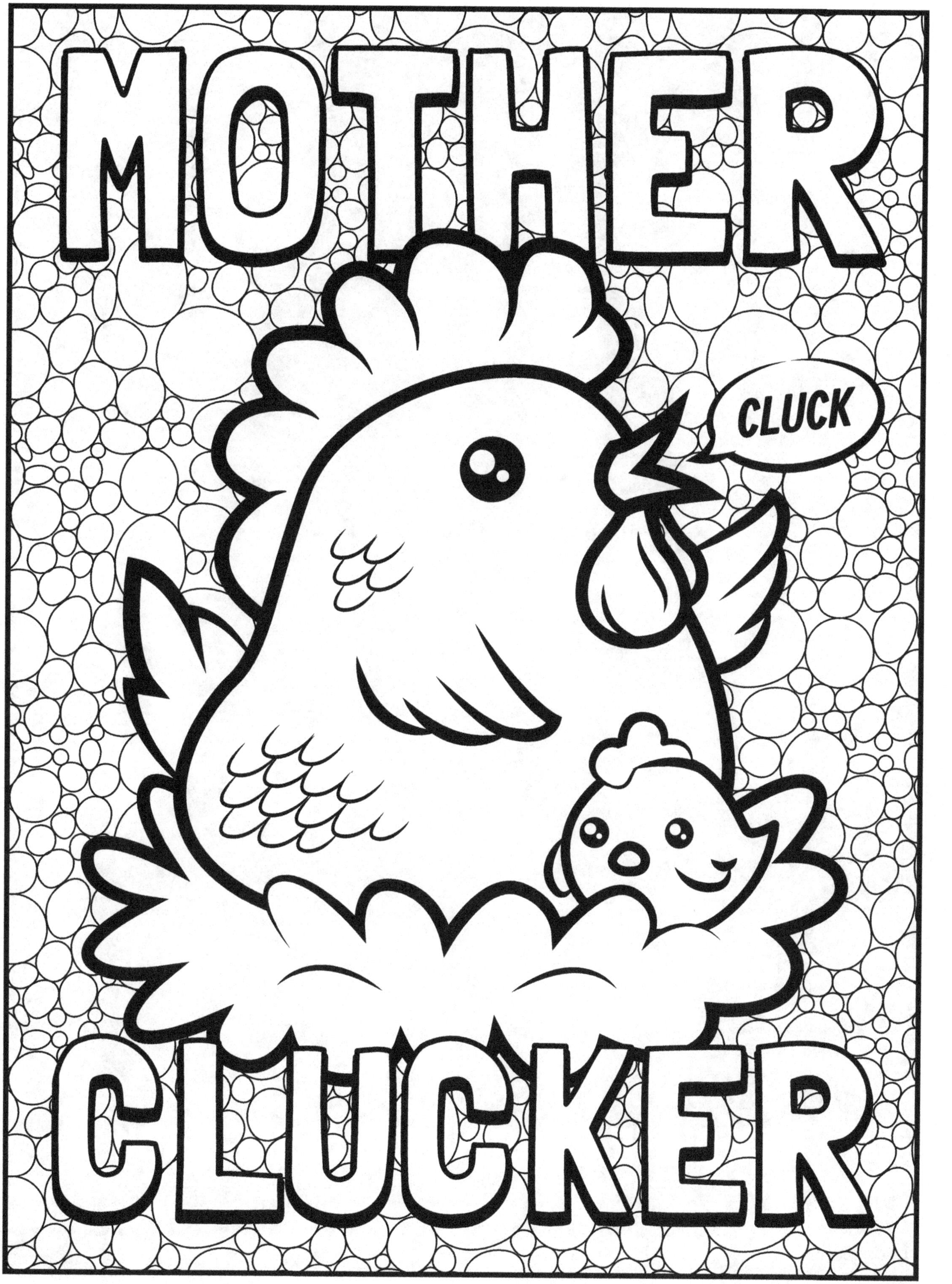
MOTHER
CLUCK
CLUCKER

NOT QUITE CUSSING COLORING BOOK

© Leafy Design. All rights reserved. No part of this publication may be reproduced, distributed or transmitted in any form or by any means including photocopying, recording or other electronic methods without the prior written permission of the publisher.

FOR *frogs* SAKE

NOT QUITE CUSSING COLORING BOOK
© Leafy Design. All rights reserved. No part of this publication may be reproduced, distributed or transmitted in any form or by any means including photocopying, recording or other electronic methods without the prior written permission of the publisher.

WHAT THE SUCCULENT!

NOT QUITE CUSSING COLORING BOOK

© Leafy Design. All rights reserved. No part of this publication may be reproduced, distributed or transmitted in any form or by any means including photocopying, recording or other electronic methods without the prior written permission of the publisher.

GREAT GALLOPING Grasshoppers

NOT QUITE CUSSING COLORING BOOK

© Leafy Design. All rights reserved. No part of this publication may be reproduced, distributed or transmitted in any form or by any means including photocopying, recording or other electronic methods without the prior written permission of the publisher.

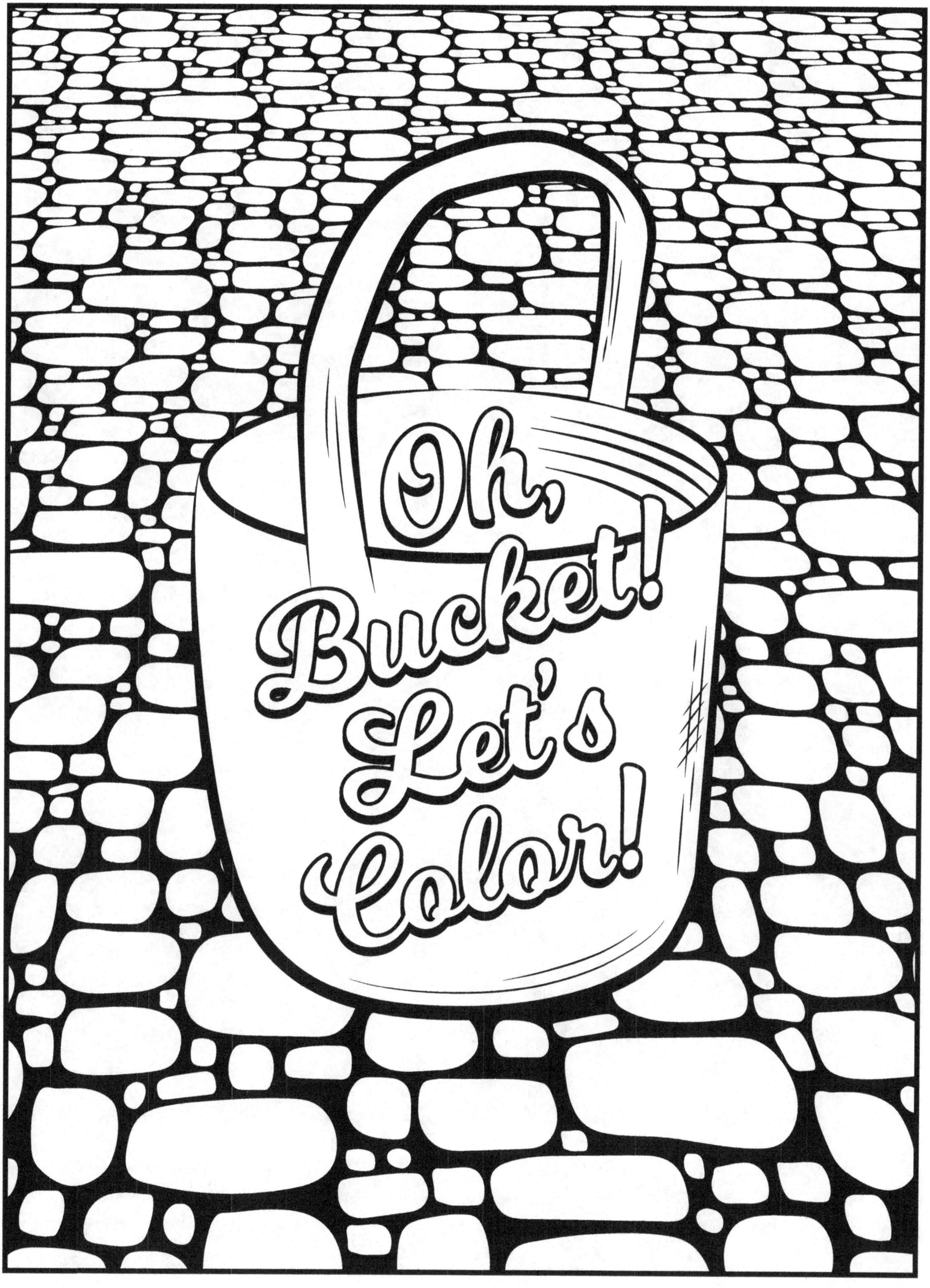
Oh,
Bucket!
Let's
Color!

NOT QUITE CUSSING COLORING BOOK

© Leafy Design. All rights reserved. No part of this publication may be reproduced, distributed or transmitted in any form or by any means including photocopying, recording or other electronic methods without the prior written permission of the publisher.

Blooming
HECK, DANG & DARNIT

NOT QUITE CUSSING COLORING BOOK

© Leafy Design. All rights reserved. No part of this publication may be reproduced, distributed or transmitted in any form or by any means including photocopying, recording or other electronic methods without the prior written permission of the publisher.

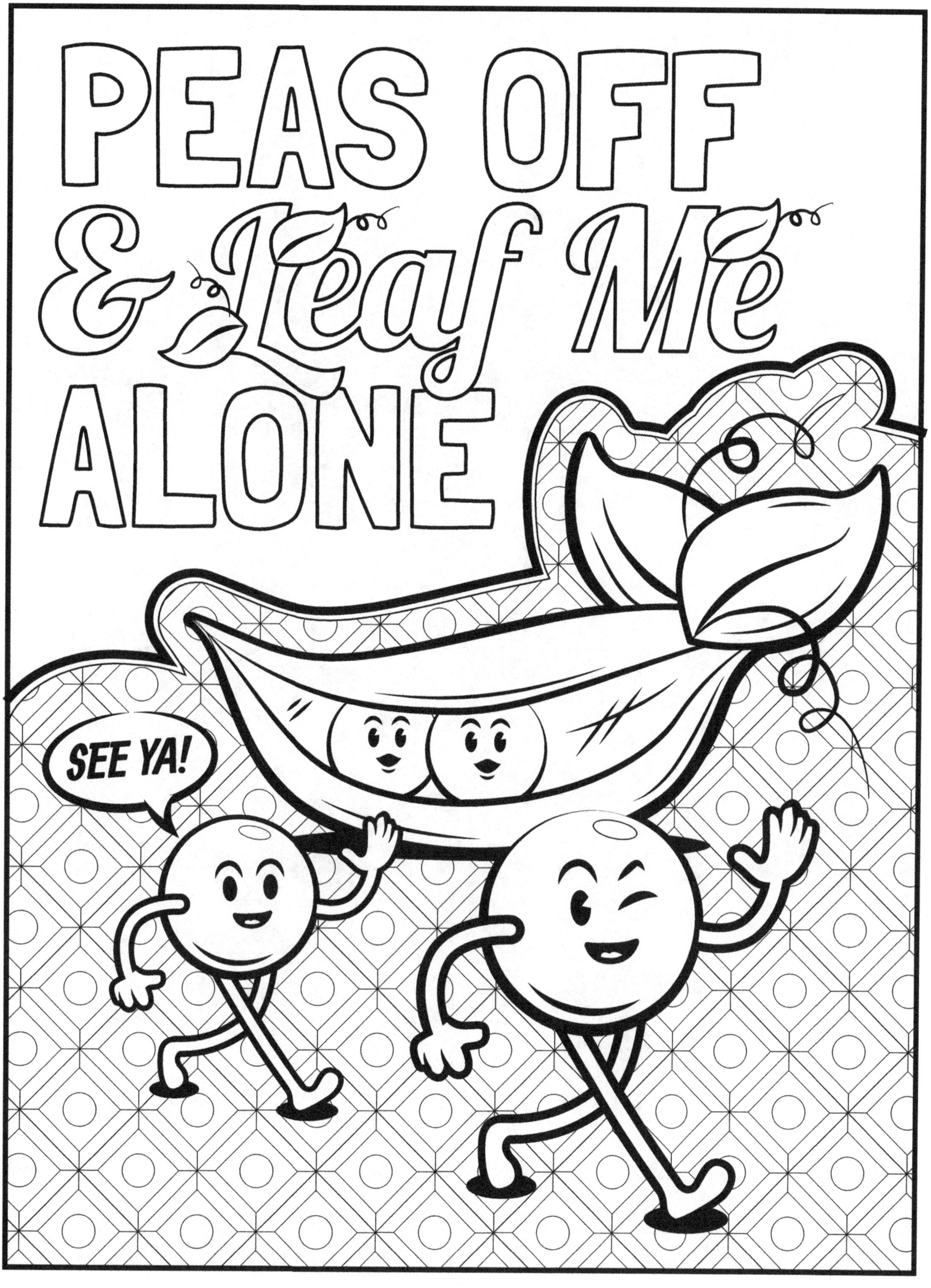
PEAS OFF
& Leaf Me
ALONE
SEE YA!

NOT QUITE CUSSING COLORING BOOK

© Leafy Design. All rights reserved. No part of this publication may be reproduced, distributed or transmitted in any form or by any means including photocopying, recording or other electronic methods without the prior written permission of the publisher.

IDGAF
I Don't Give a Fig

NOT QUITE CUSSING COLORING BOOK
© Leafy Design. All rights reserved. No part of this publication may be reproduced, distributed or transmitted in any form or by any means including photocopying, recording or other electronic methods without the prior written permission of the publisher.

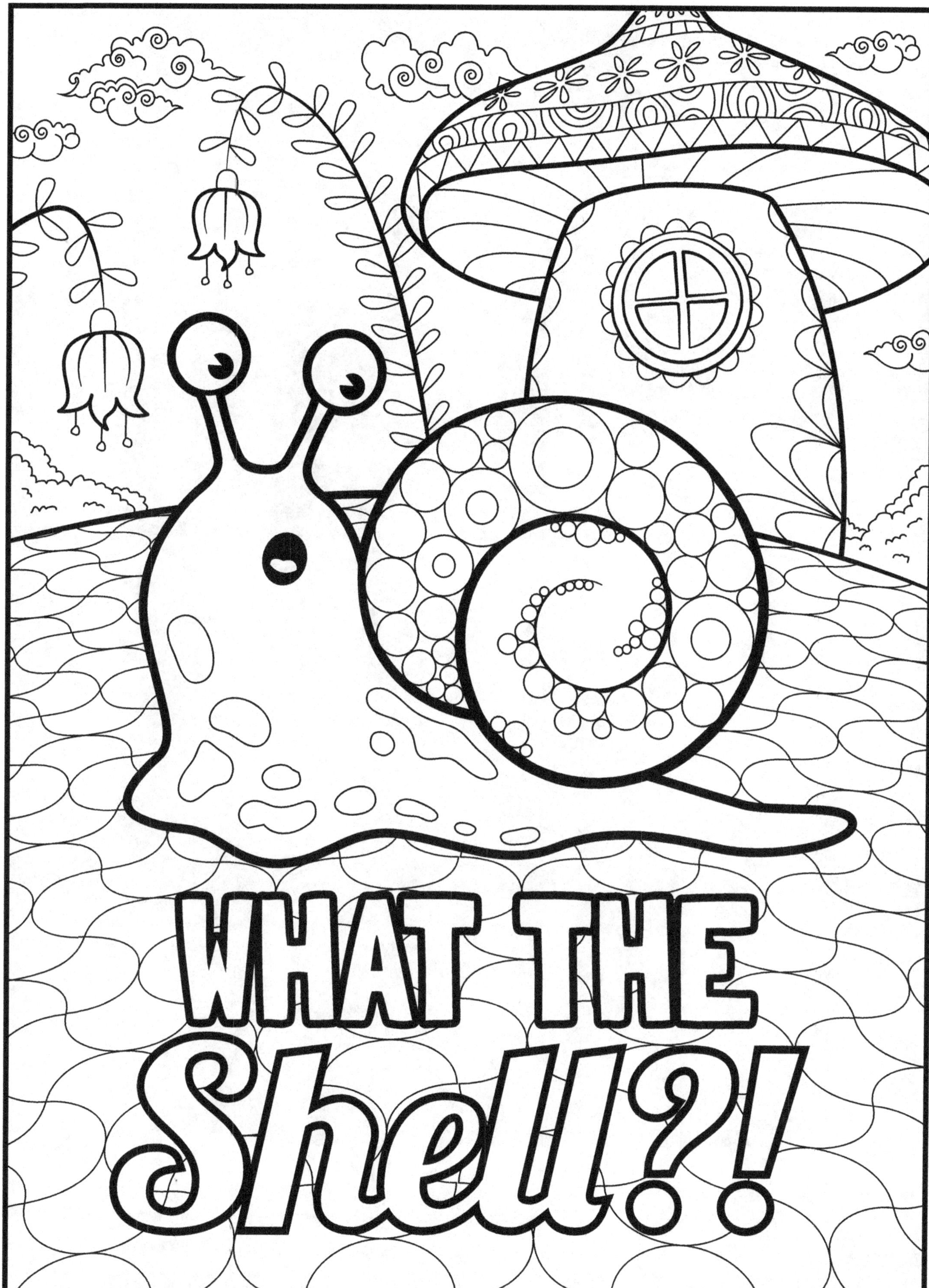
WHAT THE
Shell?!

NOT QUITE CUSSING COLORING BOOK

© Leafy Design. All rights reserved. No part of this publication may be reproduced, distributed or transmitted in any form or by any means including photocopying, recording or other electronic methods without the prior written permission of the publisher.

Made in the USA
Columbia, SC
28 November 2023